FANDOM FEVER

JUSTIN BIEBER'S BELIEBERS

BY VIRGINIA LOH-HAGAN

45TH PARALLEL PRESS

Published in the United States of America by
Cherry Lake Publishing Group
Ann Arbor, Michigan
www.cherrylakepublishing.com

Reading Adviser: Beth Walker Gambro, MS, Ed., Reading Consultant, Yorkville, IL
Content Adviser: Grace Price
Book Designer: Joseph Hatch

Photo Credits: Doug Peters/Alamy Stock Photo, cover, title page; © Jack Fordyce/Shutterstock, 4; © Debby Wong/Shutterstock, 7; © Tinseltown/Shutterstock, 8; © Debby Wong/Shutterstock, 11; © Andrea Raffin/Shutterstock, 12; © Debby Wong/Shutterstock, 13; © Debby Wong/Shutterstock, 14; © Debby Wong/Shutterstock, 17; © Debby Wong/Shutterstock, 19; © Wirestock Creators/Shutterstock, 21; © DFree/Shutterstock, 22; © Jaguar PS/Shutterstock, 25; © ZUMA Press, Inc./Alamy Stock Photo, 26; © Jack Fordyce/Shutterstock, 29; © Everett Collection/Shutterstock, 31

45th Parallel Press is an imprint of Cherry Lake Publishing Group.

Library of Congress Cataloging-in-Publication Data

Names: Loh-Hagan, Virginia, author.
Title: Justin Bieber's Beliebers / Virginia Loh-Hagan.
Description: Ann Arbor : 45th Parallel Press, 2024. | Series: Fandom fever | Audience: Grades 4-6 | Summary: "Justin Bieber's Beliebers provides an inside look at the powerful fandom of Justin Bieber. Readers will get hooked on this hi-lo title, covering facts about and insights into the group of fans who aren't afraid to make their support of J-Beebs known"— Provided by publisher.
Identifiers: LCCN 2024009452 | ISBN 9781668947470 (hardcover) | ISBN 9781668948866 (paperback) | ISBN 9781668950388 (ebook) | ISBN 9781668954942 (pdf)
Subjects: LCSH: Bieber, Justin, 1994—Juvenile literature. | Popular music fans—Juvenile literature.
Classification: LCC ML3930.B54 L65 2024 | DDC 782.42164092—dc23/eng/20240227
LC record available at https://lccn.loc.gov/2024009452

Cherry Lake Publishing Group would like to acknowledge the work of the Partnership for 21st Century Learning, a Network of Battelle for Kids. Please visit Battelle for Kids online for more information.

Note from publisher: Websites change regularly, and their future contents are outside of our control. Supervise children when conducting any recommended online searches for extended learning opportunities.

Printed in the United States of America

Table of Contents

Dr. Virginia Loh-Hagan is an author and educator. She is currently the Director of the Asian Pacific Islander Desi American (APIDA) Center at San Diego State University and the Co-Executive Director of The Asian American Education Project. She lives in San Diego with her very tall husband and very naughty dogs.

xoxo JUSTIN

Justin Bieber is grateful to his fans. They are called Beliebers.

CHAPTER ONE

From Fan Base to Fandom

Musicians make music. They perform music. Some become big stars. They become **celebrities**. Celebrities are famous. They have a **fan base**. A fan base is a group of supporters.

Most fans have a casual interest. But some fans are more devoted. They worship their **idols**. Idols are big stars. Devoted fans form **fandoms**. Fandoms are communities. They're networks of fans.

Fandoms of musicians are special groups. They buy the musicians' music. They buy their **merch**. Merch means merchandise. It means stuff that can be sold. Merch includes shirts and posters. Fans follow musicians on tour. They attend their shows. They go on tour with them. They connect with the music. They connect with the messages. They sing their songs. They know all the words.

Fandoms are a powerful force. They can influence music. They use the internet. The internet gives fans information about their idols. It gives them more access to their idols. It also gives them more access to other fans.

Fans build relationships with each other. They share their knowledge. They share their passion. They build connections. They create content. They share content.

Fans make fan art. This is when they draw pictures of their idols. Fans also write stories about their idols. This is called fan fiction. They share their art. They share their stories.

Some celebrities have large fandoms. Their fandoms even have special names. That's a sign of success!

Justin Bieber's popularity has been called "Bieber Fever."

Justin Bieber was raised by a single mother.

CHAPTER TWO

Fanning Justin Bieber

Justin Bieber was born in 1994. He's a Canadian singer. He was a teen idol. He's a pop **icon**. An icon is a person or thing. An icon is admired in a certain area. He has shaped today's music. He sings different types of music.

He learned to play instruments at an early age. In 2007, he entered a singing contest. He was 12. He got second place. It was his mother who made him famous. She posted a video of his performance. She did this on YouTube. Bieber became a hit.

His songs are top hits. He performs all around the world. His shows sell out. He always has big crowds. He's sold more than 150 million albums. He's won many awards. His fandom is known as the Beliebers.

Belieber combines 2 words. The 2 words are Bieber and believer. These fans believe in Bieber. They support him. They defend him.

Beliebers formed around 2009. They formed after seeing Bieber's YouTube videos. He was the first person to hit 2 billion views on his videos.

At first, his fans were mostly teen girls. Bieber's talent improved. He sang more songs. He became more famous. There were boy Beliebers. There were older Beliebers. Today, there are more than 67 million Beliebers.

Loving Bieber is called "Bieber Fever." Many fans crush on him. They send him love letters. They collect merch. They collect pictures. They use these things to build **shrines**. These are places devoted to a person or religious figure.

Beliebers were pioneers in online engagement.

SUPER FAN

In 2018, Bieber married Hailey Baldwin. They had a secret wedding. But their marriage is very public. Hailey is a model. Her father is actor Stephen Baldwin. Bieber wrote a song about her. The song is called "Hailey." He said, "We'll be diamond when our golden days are done." Hailey is a Belieber. Bieber posted a picture of Hailey. He wrote, "People always asked me if I'd marry a Belieber. Well, I did!!!" Hailey tried to deny it. She said, "I was never a superfan, of him or anyone. It was never that crazed, screaming thing. I didn't think about it in any kind of way except for the fact that he was cute. Everybody had a crush on him." Over the years, she has posted positive comments. She liked his hair. She praised his songs. Then, they got serious. Hailey said, "He's somebody I really cherish."

Bieber connected to his fans. He said, “I love all my fans.” He answers their questions. He creates contests. Contest winners get special prizes. They can meet him backstage. They can buy his show tickets before others.

The best prize is when Bieber follows fans back on social media. Beliebers hope for direct contact. They want Bieber to follow them back. They want a direct message.

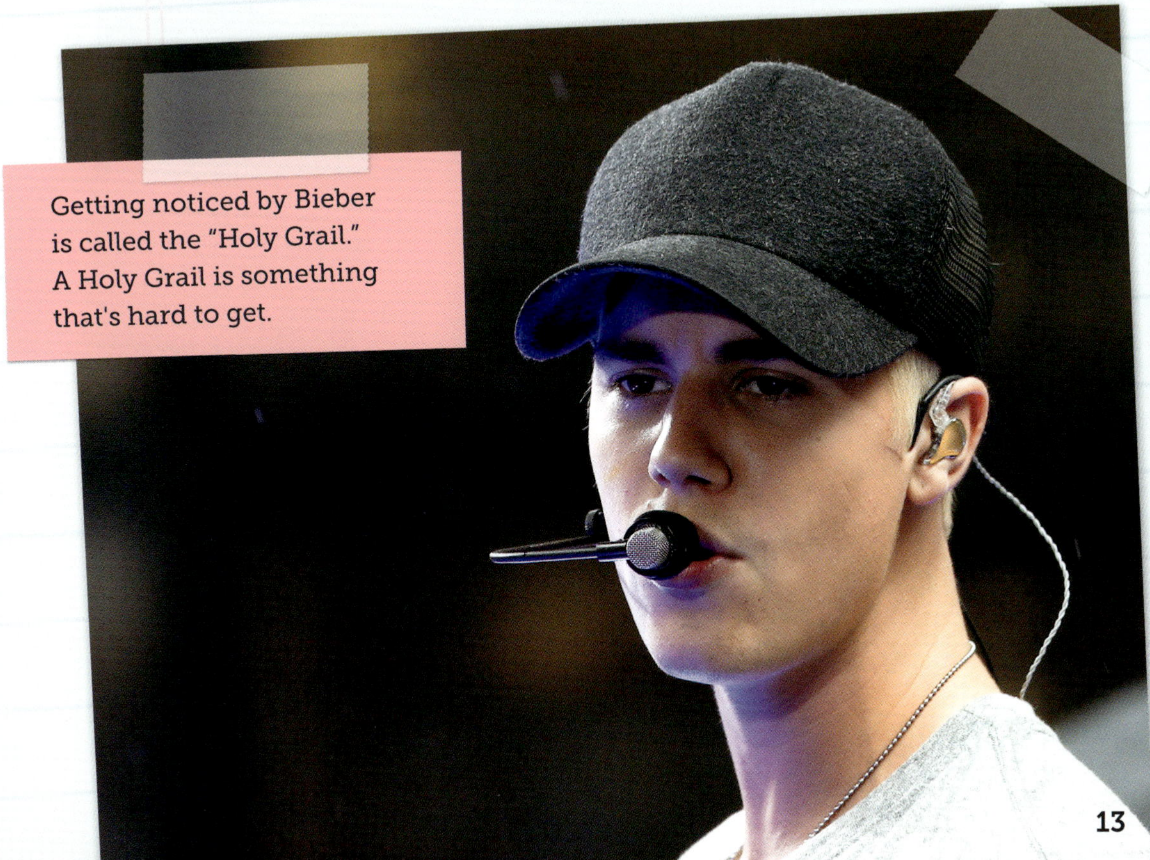

Getting noticed by Bieber is called the "Holy Grail." A Holy Grail is something that's hard to get.

Make signs. Add funny messages to your outfit. An example is "I have Bieber Fever."

CHAPTER THREE

Living That Fan Life

Beliebers show up at Justin Bieber events. To be a Belieber, make sure to look the part! Do the following:

+ Wear T-shirts. Find different ways to style them.
+ Wear plaid shirts. Wear T-shirts underneath. This is a "skater" look.
+ Wear sports team clothes. Wear baseball caps. Bieber is a sports fan. He likes basketball. He likes hockey.
+ Wear a hoodie. A hoodie is a sweatshirt with a hood.
+ Wear casual bottoms. Wear baggy shorts. Wear jeans.
+ Wear sneakers.
+ Layer your look. Wear several clothing items. Wear hats or beanies. Wear long necklaces. Wear sunglasses.
+ Add purple to your outfit. Bieber's favorite color is purple.

Beliebers have their own culture. To be a Belieber, make sure to act the part! Do the following:

+ Organize. Connect with other fans. Buy tickets to Bieber's shows. Help sell out his shows.

+ Memorize his song **lyrics**. Lyrics are the words to songs. Beliebers can sing along. They know all his songs.

+ Recreate Bieber's music videos. Post them. Share the Bieber love.

+ Help Bieber fans meet Bieber while he's on tour. This project is called Beliebers Help Beliebers.

+ Create fan accounts. Post a lot on social media.

+ Respect his crew members, like his bodyguard, Kenny.

Justin Bieber is known for being a hard worker. He puts his all into his music and performances.

Fanatic Fan

Dylan Desclos is French. He looks like Bieber. He dresses like him. He has the same tattoos. He said they also share the same attitudes. He said, "I became a look-alike simply by going to a Justin Bieber concert. I took a lot of photos, and I thought it was super cool." He performs as Bieber. He does this on stage. He sings his songs. He posts videos. He said, "...when I'm onstage, I need to be the most Justin I can be. And I think I'm good at mimicking him." He mimics Bieber when Bieber is not touring. He helps fill in the time between releases. He gets mobbed. Beliebers think he's the real Bieber. Desclos said, "I would say the best and funniest reaction I got was people thinking I was Justin and knocking on my hotel door at 2 a.m." Some Beliebers don't like him. A fan said, "Stop trying to be someone you're not." Another fan said, "I don't find it funny how this guy tries to be Justin. He lives off it."

Not all fan behavior is good. Some fans can be **toxic**. Toxic means harmful. To be a Belieber, don't let your passion become poison. Do the following:

+ Respect Bieber's privacy. Toxic fans have stalked him. They've broken into his house. They've broken into his hotel rooms. Dana Martin is a toxic fan. He has a tattoo of Bieber on his right leg. He hired 2 people to hurt Bieber. He was sent to jail.

+ Don't mess with Bieber's social media. A hater reported Bieber. He said Bieber's videos were violating **copyright** laws. Copyrights are legal rights of content owners. This was a lie. But Bieber's videos were taken down. So the prank worked. But the videos were put back up soon after.

People have a right to live their lives. Focus on the art more than the artist.

It's okay to be a passionate Belieber. Just don't be toxic.

CHAPTER FOUR

The Power of Fandom

Beliebers are inspired by their idol. They support him. They support his causes. Together, they're a powerful force. They've helped people. They've made social changes.

Some Beliebers host Bieber Buyouts. They organize on social media. They meet at malls. They buy all things related to Bieber. They increase Bieber's sales. They also donate the items to **charity**. A charity is a group that helps people in need. Mani Ahluwalia is a Belieber. She hosted a Bieber Buyout. She said, "...a lot of kids at SickKids are huge fans of Justin." SickKids is a Canadian hospital for children.

Beliebers mostly connect online. Bieber Buyouts give them a chance to meet up in real life.

In 2011, Bieber held a charity drive. He called it Believe. He also released a Christmas album. He said he'd donate a part of the sales to Believe. He asked his fans to do the same. He chose charities that supported education, youth well-being, and music. He said, "...I know firsthand that if you believe in your dreams, everything is possible...donate as little as one dollar. Or even donate your time. Because everything will make a difference...I know that with your help we can make a change."

Bieber shared his struggles. He talked about mental health. He talked about his problems. This made fans feel closer to him. This made fans feel more open. Fans felt like they weren't alone. Many fans sent him thank-you notes. They helped each other feel safer.

Bieber has donated money to his local food bank. He said, "I actually used to get food from there."

Idol Inspiration

Idols have idols. Bieber admires Black artists. He said they have shaped his sound. He said, "I am inspired by Black culture. I have benefited off of Black culture. My style, how I sing, dance, perform, and my fashion have all been influenced by Black culture." He said, "Music is music. And I'm definitely influenced by Michael Jackson and Boyz II Men and people who were Black artists...I like their voices and I like how they entertain..." Boyz II Men is an American band. They have great harmony. They sing well together. They sing emotional songs. Bieber asked them to appear on his holiday album. This happened in 2011. Bieber has covered their songs. He sang "End of the Road." Bieber said, "I am committed to using my platform...to learn, to speak up about racial justice..."

CHAPTER FIVE

Insider Information

Fans know their idols. They can also spot fake fans. Make sure you do your research. Here are the top 10 things every true Belieber should know about Justin Bieber!

1. Bieber signed his first recording contract at age 13. Usher is a rapper. He signed Bieber. Justin Timberlake is also a singer. He wanted to sign Bieber as well. Bieber's first song was "One Time."

2. Bieber released "Baby." He did this at age 15. The song was a number-one hit.

3. Bieber got his first tattoo at age 16. He has more than 60 tattoos. He has them all over his body. But he won't tattoo his hands. His favorite tattoo is a bear.

Usher mentored Justin Bieber. Justin Bieber looks up to him.

Bieber has faced negative drama. Beliebers defended him.

4. Bieber bought his family a house. He did this at age 19. He had grown up poor. He used his money to help his family.

5. Bieber started his own clothing line. The company is called Drew House. It's named after his middle name. It sells clothes. It sells jewelry. It's **unisex**. Unisex means designed for all genders.

6. Bieber had a pet monkey. He brought it on tour. He took it to Germany. German officials took the monkey. The monkey was taken to a zoo.

7. Bieber stays in shape while touring. He has 2 big tour buses. He said, "I have a studio bus and a workout bus. It's just a big gym."

8. Bieber is active on social media. But he doesn't text. He doesn't even have a cell phone. He lives his life without one.

9. Bieber has a fear of small spaces. He's had this fear since age 7. He hates elevators. He hates clowns. He also dislikes cats. He once dreamed a cat ate him.

10. Bieber's favorite sandwich is tomato and mayo on white bread. His favorite animal is a giraffe.

There's so much more to learn! Make sure to keep up with the latest.

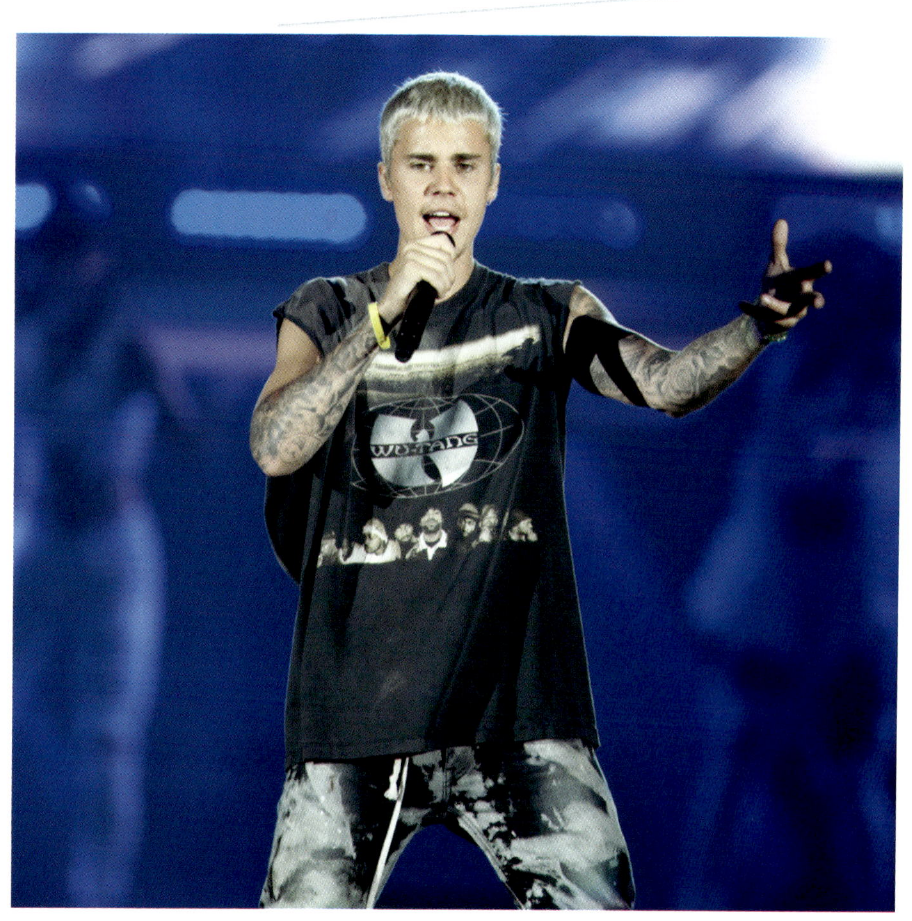

Bieber's last tour was the Justice World Tour. The one before that was the Purpose World Tour.

Fans have their own language. Here are some Belieber words you should know:

- **BIEBERculosis:** This word means a love curse. It describes a feeling of being in love with Bieber.
- **Bieber Fever:** This describes the effect Bieber has over people.
- **Bieber-Hater:** People who hate Bieber.
- **Bieberholic:** Fans who need to engage with Bieber every day.
- **Bieberish:** Feeling lovesick. It refers to having a romantic crush.
- **BieberMania:** Describes screaming fans at a show.
- **Bieberphobia:** Bieberphobia is a fear of Bieber. It refers to haters.
- **Bieberty:** Bieber has been a star since he was young. He became a teenager in the public eye. Bieberty refers to Bieber's puberty. It's when he became a young adult.
- **Biebette:** A girl who's obsessed with Bieber.

Bieber loves his fans. He said, "I don't think of myself as powerful. If anything, my fans are powerful. It's all in their hands. If they don't buy my albums, I go away."

Fans love when Bieber mentions them. He said, "...I just want to thank all my fans...this is not just my award, this is my whole Belieber fan group-nation." He also said, "The media talks a lot about me. They make up a lot of lies and want me to fail. But, I'm never leaving you. Being a Belieber is a lifestyle."

There are all types of Beliebers. Beliebers are all around the world. Start your own fan club!

- Promote your fan club.
- Collect a list of names.
- Plan events.
- Host a meeting.
- Have fun!

Beliebers grew up with Justin Bieber. Bieber has been performing since he was young. He has gone through many changes.

GLOSSARY

celebrities (suh-LEH-bruh-teez) well-known or famous people

charity (CHAIR-uh-tee) organization set up to provide help and raise money for those in need

copyright (KAH-pee-riyt) legal right that protects original works from being copied

fan base (FAN BAYSS) group of fans for a particular sport, musical group, or celebrity

fandom (FAN-duhm) subculture, community, or network of fans who share a common interest

icon (IYE-kaan) a person or thing widely admired in a particular area

idols (EYE-duhlz) people who are greatly admired and loved by others

lyrics (LEER-iks) words to songs

merch (MURCH) short for merchandise, which includes posters, shirts, and other items

shrine (SHRYN) place created to honor a person or a religious figure

toxic (TAHK-sik) harmful

unisex (YOO-nuh-seks) designed for all genders

LEARN MORE

Higgins, Nadia. *Justin Bieber: Pop and R & B Idol.* Minneapolis, MN: Lerner Publications, 2013.

MacDonald, Barry. *Everything Real Justin Bieber Fans Should Know & Do.* Chicago, IL: Triumph Books, 2012.

Wilcox, Christine. *Justin Bieber.* Detroit, MI: Lucent Books, 2013.

INDEX